Dial Books for Young Readers

Penguin Young Readers Group

An imprint of Penguin Random House LLC

375 Hudson Street, New York, NY 10014

Printed in China • ISBN 9780525555452 • 10 9 8 7 6 5 4 3 2 1

Design by Lily Malcom • Text set in Sentinel

JON AGEE

THE WALL IN THE MIDDLE OF THE BOOK

There's a wall in the middle of the book.

And it's a good thing.

The wall protects this side of the book . . .

from the other side of the book.

This side of the book is safe.

The other side is not.

But the most dangerous thing
on the other side of the book
is the ogre.

If the ogre ever caught me, he'd eat me up.

That's why I'm glad there's a wall
in the middle of the book,
and that I'm on this side of it.

Wait a second. What's going on?!

This is not supposed to happen
on this side of the wall!

Wow!
Thank you so much!

OH NO!
I'm on the other side of the book!

And you're the ogre who's going to eat me up!

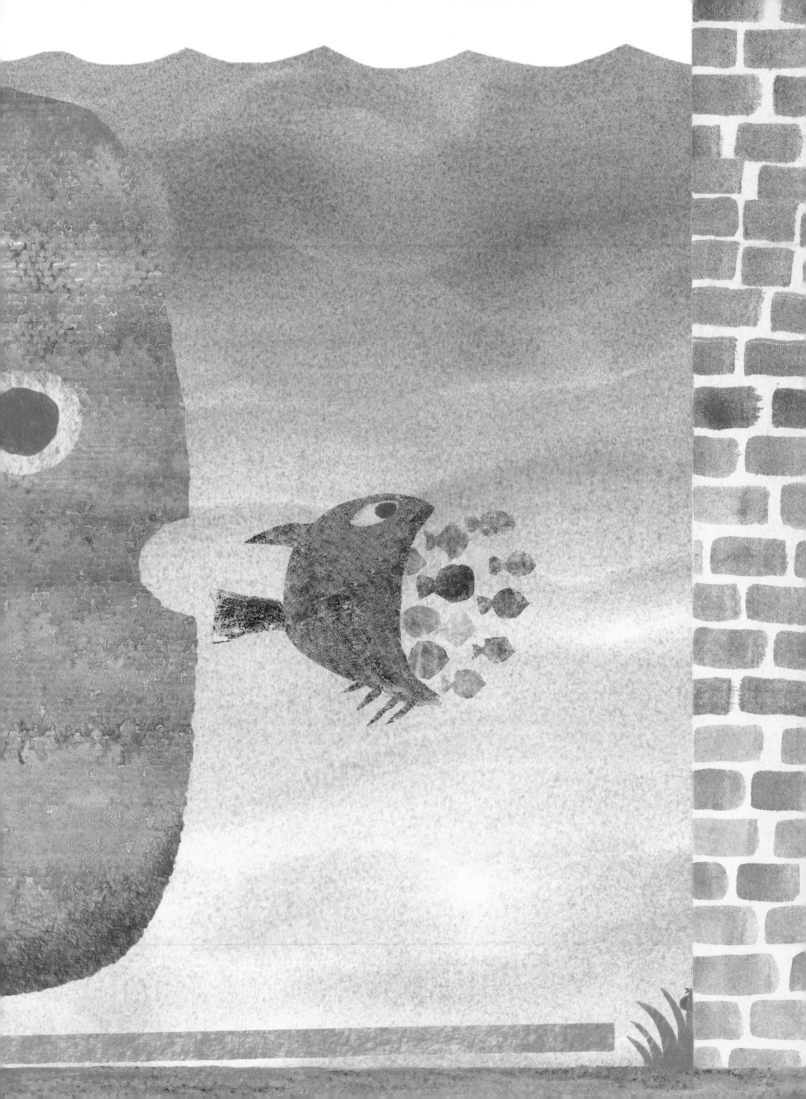

Haw-haw-haw! I'm actually a nice ogre.
And this side of the book is fantastic!

C'mon, I'll show you around!

Hey, ogre! Wait for me!